TRUMPETS
in
GRUMPETLAND

PETER CROSS
STORY BY
PETER DALLAS-SMITH

RANDOM HOUSE 🏠 NEW YORK

First American Edition, 1985.
Illustrations copyright © 1984 by Peter Cross.
Text copyright © 1984 by Peter Dallas-Smith.
All rights reserved under International and
Pan-American Copyright Conventions.
Published in the United States by Random House, Inc.,
New York, and simultaneously in Canada by Random House
of Canada Limited, Toronto. Originally published in
England by A & C Black (Publishers) Ltd., London.

Library of Congress Cataloging in Publication Data:
Cross, Peter. Trumpets in Grumpetland.
SUMMARY: Livingstone the lute player and the
beautiful Kim are brought together by their love
of music, while fierce Havoc the Grumpet and his
Grumpicats are repelled, at least temporarily, by
the Trumpets and the Borderers. 1. Children's
stories, English. [1. Fantasy]
I. Dallas-Smith, Peter.
II. Title. PZ7.C88274Tru 1985
[Fic] 84-11491
ISBN: 0-394-87028-X (trade); 0-394-97028-4 (lib. bdg.)
Manufactured in Italy by A. Mondadori — Verona
1 2 3 4 5 6 7 8 9 0

It was a fine sunny morning and Hortensia, Queen of Trumpets, was feeding her ducklings. Like all Trumpets, she was a warm and friendly person; but she was a Queen, too, to the tips of her paws, and Grumpets made her cross. Grumpets were a nuisance. They were cold, bossy creatures, always trying to make trouble

and especially trouble for Trumpets.

3

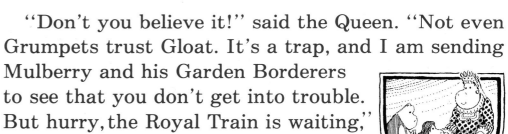

That very morning,
Livingstone, the Queen's lute player,
and his friend Podd were leaving on
a journey up to Grumpet country.

When Livingstone's beautiful old lute had
been broken last summer, a strange Grumpet called Gloat
had lent him another one — a poor, square thing which Gloat had
promised to replace with something better.

"Don't you believe it!" said the Queen. "Not even
Grumpets trust Gloat. It's a trap, and I am sending
Mulberry and his Garden Borderers
to see that you don't get into trouble.
But hurry, the Royal Train is waiting,"
and she held out her paw
for them to kiss.

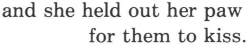

As the train swept silently through the dark tunnels of Deep Down, the Trumpets' own underground railway, Mulberry unrolled his map. On one side were the Eastlands, belonging to the mysterious Greygown, whom few Trumpets had met; on the other side, everything belonged to Havoc, a very fierce Grumpet indeed.

MULBERRY'S MAP

THE NORTH (HAVOC'S WORLD)

EAST LANDS

PEAK OF HYHAT

NORTH CIRCULAR

BEN-BROS 3;2¹²

GRUMPIAN MTS.

GREYGOWN

EAST LANDS ROAD

NORTH FORK

ROCKING STONE

GREYGOWN'S SUMMER LODGE

GORGE OF GRUMPETS

WINTERFOLD FOREST

THE RASPBERRY PLANTATION

BORDER COUNTRY

NORTHGATE

N E W S

THINK TANK

?

TO AND FROM KENTISH TOWN

MARY ROSE

"Keep away from Havoc whatever you do," Mulberry told Podd, "and remember, we Borderers will not be far away, if you need us."
Livingstone, half listening, dreamed in his corner of his old lost lute.

All the way to Northgate they went, up in the Border country, where the tall trees took their breath away and the Grumpet Mountains seemed horribly close. A buggy was waiting, drawn by a fine rabbit called Hercules. Podd and Livingstone jumped aboard and soon they were waving good-bye to the Borderers as they drove off into the twilight.

The doors of the station closed and you would never have known that a hidden world of Trumpets lay there beneath the forest floor.

NORTHGATE

PLEASE SHOW YOUR TICKETS

It's NO TROUBLE for TRUMPETS

GRINDLEY'S BOOK & TENNIS CLUB

BOOKSELLER LOUIS BAUM

Don't forget Your WINTERWARMS!

SOUTH ROOTS TO DOWN

DEEP·DOWN
· NORTHERN LINE ·

Great Snailback

South Wibblydon

The Broadway (No Tooting after 11.00 p.m.)

Two toots Back

Lavender Hill

St Ockwell

The Oval (Vauxhall Lane)

Water Loo (Relief service)

Badgerphant & Castle

OUSEL

8

The two travelers reached North Fork, in the Gorge of Grumpets, as dawn was breaking.

All around, great stone Grumpets stared down at them through the morning mist; but they were early for their meeting with Gloat and he had not arrived. Ahead of them was a notice:

· THE GORGE OF GRUMPETS ·

Podd and Livingstone looked at each other uneasily.
"Let's take a look along the Eastlands road," said Podd.
"We can still be back in time to meet Gloat."

THE EASTLANDS ROAD

They had not gone far when Livingstone heard the distant sound of a lute. It seemed to come from a great stone some way off.

They unhitched the buggy and climbed toward the sound. Livingstone caught hold of the topmost ledge and was just starting to haul himself up when the heavy boulder tilted toward him, rocking on its base.

Instantly the music stopped and as Livingstone struggled to hold on, two cloaked figures appeared above him.

"Who are you?"
a stern voice demanded.
Livingstone steadied himself on Podd's
shoulders and gave his name.
The taller figure leaned forward
in surprise. "Livingstone
the lute player?" he asked. "I am
delighted to meet you, sir.
My name is Greygown and
this is my daughter, Kim."

Livingstone noticed her beautiful old
lute, so like the one he had lost,
then looked up at Kim.

Neither of them spoke. Yet when Kim finally lowered her gaze
... Livingstone was already in love!

Meanwhile a balloon was fast approaching behind them. Its occupant was waving

excitedly and Podd soon recognized the black eye patch of Gloat the Grumpet.

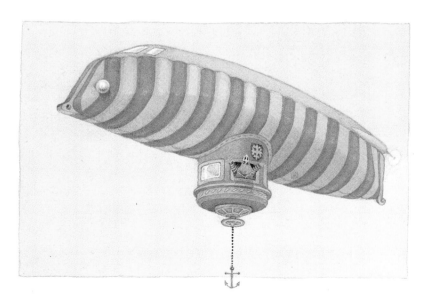 

They could hear him shouting . . .

Greygown!
Greygown! Your daughter is in danger. Havoc the Chief is coming. He wants to take her away and marry her and . . . .

Balloon weevil

As Gloat's voice trailed away, Podd was calling Mulberry on Trumpet Band Radio:

Stand by for trouble

At that very moment Havoc was pacing the floor of his secret hangar, deep inside the Peak of Hyhat.

Work on his new Grumpicat squadron had finished at last and everywhere Grumpets stood watching him, waiting for orders.

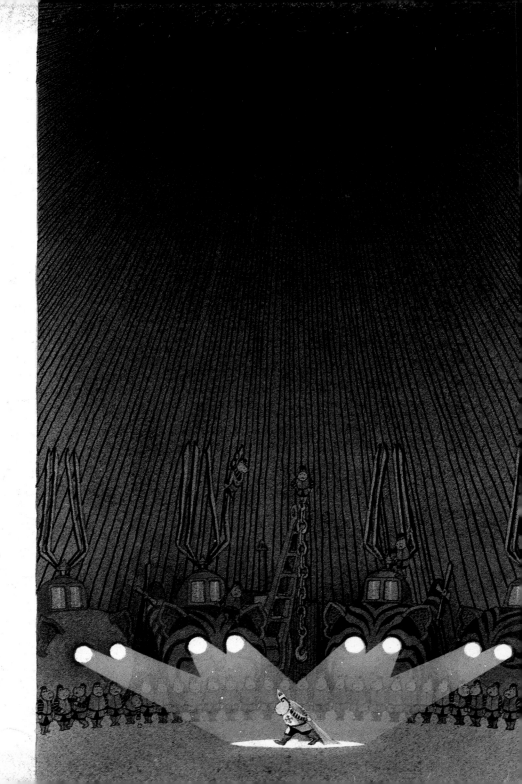

Suddenly Havoc swung around.
"Prepare for launch!" he barked —
and listened to the great capstan
starting to turn.

Soon the launch pad was worming
its way upward and slowly
the Lid of Hyhat began to open . . .

Havoc had always dreamed of marrying Kim.
With her as his wife, he would be able
to count on Greygown's support —
and that would make him the
most powerful lord in all the
Borderlands. Even the rich
and sunny Land of
Trumpets would
then be within
his grasp.

Havoc's eyes gleamed.
    Now was the time for action! His paw came down,
        fierce as a karate chop, signaling the Grumpicats into the air.

Starling sky-spies reported to Havoc whenever Greygown and Kim visited their summer lodge in the hills and now, as Havoc wheeled his squadron across the sky, he knew exactly where he was going.

Over the Gorge of Grumpets he flew
— and saw a strange-looking
buggy driving hard for the
Trumpet Border.

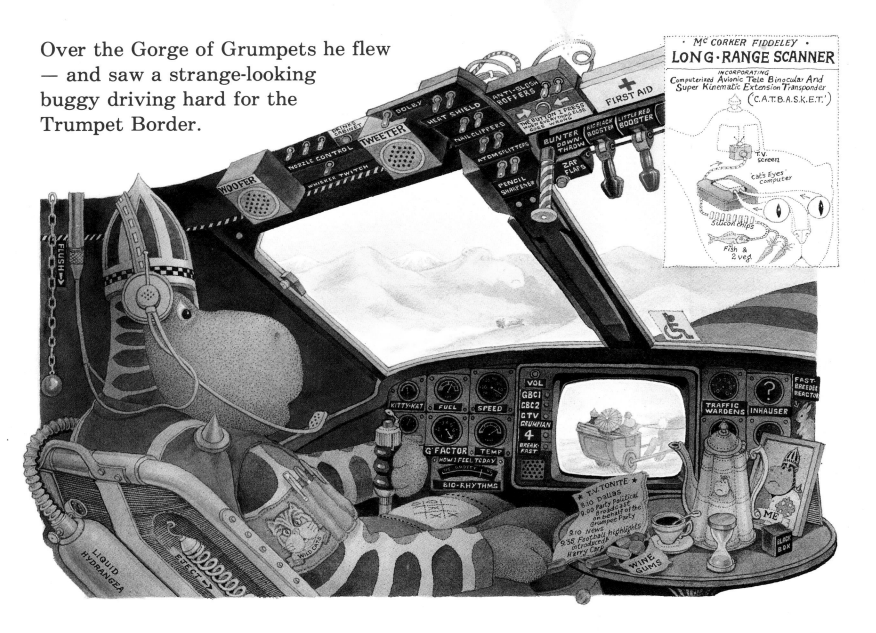

His long-range scanner showed it up clearly and there, in the back, was a parasol
— Kim's parasol. With a snarl, Havoc banked steeply and gave chase.

Podd heard the roar in the sky behind him. "Grumpicats! Grumpicats! Gaining ground by the second," he radioed, and above the din just caught Mulberry's reply: "Head for the raspberries. Head for the . . ."

"STOP!" bellowed Havoc in triumph. Three faces looked up at him.
Not one of them was Kim's. Furiously Havoc turned, but it was too late.

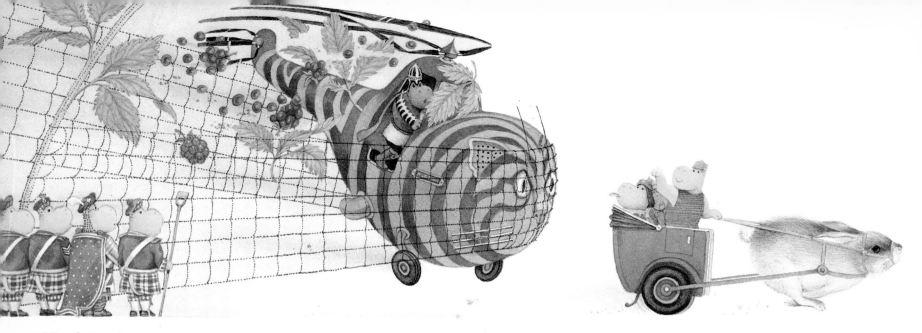

He hit the netting with stunning force; as the cords stretched like elastic, Havoc slowed . . .
stopped . . .

and then to his horror found himself being hurled back, faster and faster,
straight at his own squadron!

The Great Grumpicatastrophe.

Through all the confusion, Podd and Hercules managed somehow to bring the buggy to a stop beneath the safety of the raspberry canes.

The Borderers cheered — and cheered again as the trunk opened and Kim stepped gracefully out.

Havoc heard the cheering as he clambered aboard a Rescue Grumpicat, and Mulberry was glad to see him go. Captured Grumpets were always a problem and already some of his Borderers had spotted Gloat, dangling from his collapsed balloon. But before they could bring him in, a Royal Messenger arrived and ran panting to Mulberry.

"Her Majesty," he gasped, "requests the pleasure of your company . . . at Northgate, now!"

Everyone who saw it long remembered the meeting between Greygown and Queen Hortensia. Each was as gracious as the other and the gentle Kim touched everyone with her charm.